Walt Disney
AMERICAN CL
Little Hiawatha

Twin Books

MALLARD PRESS

Little Hiawatha was both excited and scared. This was his first hunting trip, and he was far from home. He had just spun dizzily through the great falls of Minnehaha and landed safely in a quiet pool.

With one foot on the bank and the other in his little birchbark canoe, he shaded his eyes like a fearless warrior, looked about him—and almost fell into the water! The animals who had gathered to watch him land began to laugh.

Angrily, Little Hiawatha jumped ashore and pointed his bow and arrow. "Think it's funny, do you?" he demanded, struggling to pull back his bowstring. The squirrels, rabbits, raccoons, and other animals ran for cover.

"You'd better run!" shouted Little Hiawatha. "A fierce warrior from the far north is here to hunt you!" He sounded so scary that he almost scared himself.

Then a loud stomping sound caught his attention, and he froze. Surely, some great beast of the forest was coming. He dropped to the ground to listen for its footsteps, as a skillful hunter would.

Thump, thump, thump—the beast was coming closer! Wide-eyed with excitement, Little Hiawatha pressed his ear closer to the ground. Suddenly, a great big grasshopper landed right beside him!

"*Yikes!*" yelled Little Hiawatha, jumping as high as the grasshopper. It took off again, in another long leap, and Little Hiawatha tried to aim his bow and arrow in midair. But the grasshopper was too fast for him. Another great leap brought it to a pile of rocks. Hoping to catch up, Little Hiawatha hopped after the grasshopper.

By this time, all the little animals that had run away were peeking out from behind the trees. One rabbit, bolder than the others, had just hopped onto a tree stump when Little Hiawatha tripped and fell flat! The grasshopper whizzed away, and the little rabbit burst out laughing. He laughed so hard he had to hold his furry sides, and all the other animals laughed with him!

Little Hiawatha was very angry when he got up! Not only had he lost the grasshopper—all the animals he had come to hunt were laughing at him. Glaring, he moved towards the little rabbit with his bow and arrow.

The other animals looked frightened, and the rabbit stopped laughing and shrank away. But it was too late for him to run. Little Hiawatha was very close.

Shocked and scared, the other animals watched Little
Hiawatha draw closer to the tree stump. The trapped rabbit
was shaking with fright. He was about to cry.

Suddenly, Little Hiawatha didn't feel much like a mighty
hunter. He stopped and lowered his bow and arrow. Then *he*
started to cry.

Angrily, Little Hiawatha broke his arrow in half. All the animals came out of hiding to cheer him, and the little rabbit hopped quickly to his family. Meanwhile, Little Hiawatha's headband had fallen over his eyes, so he didn't see the enormous bear track on the ground beside him!

When he pushed the headband back up, Little Hiawatha noticed the huge track. Open-mouthed, he stared at it. This might be his chance to be a great hunter, after all! This bear must be the biggest in all the forest, and he would track it down. What stories he would have to tell when he got home! Excitedly, Little Hiawatha dropped to the ground to stalk the bear on hands and knees.

Little Hiawatha was so intent on his stalking that he didn't see the bear cub that came out from behind a tree to sniff the tracks.

Carefully, Little Hiawatha crept along the ground toward
the edge of the clearing. Any minute now, he might catch
sight of the great bear. But suddenly, he and the cub bumped
heads!

Both of them were so frightened that they ran in opposite directions! But Little Hiawatha turned back to see if he was being followed. He spotted the cub kicking up little puffs of dust as it raced through the woods.

Little Hiawatha spun around and chased the cub through the trees, ducking low branches and dodging moss-covered rocks.

Breathless, the cub safely reached his mother, who was sleeping under a tree. He jumped onto her back and slid down her side to hide behind her. And right behind him was Little Hiawatha, who didn't realize for a second that he had jumped up on top of the big bear!

The mother bear opened her eyes and looked around for the enemy who had frightened her cub. Feeling Little Hiawatha's weight on her back, she lumbered to her feet and shook him off.

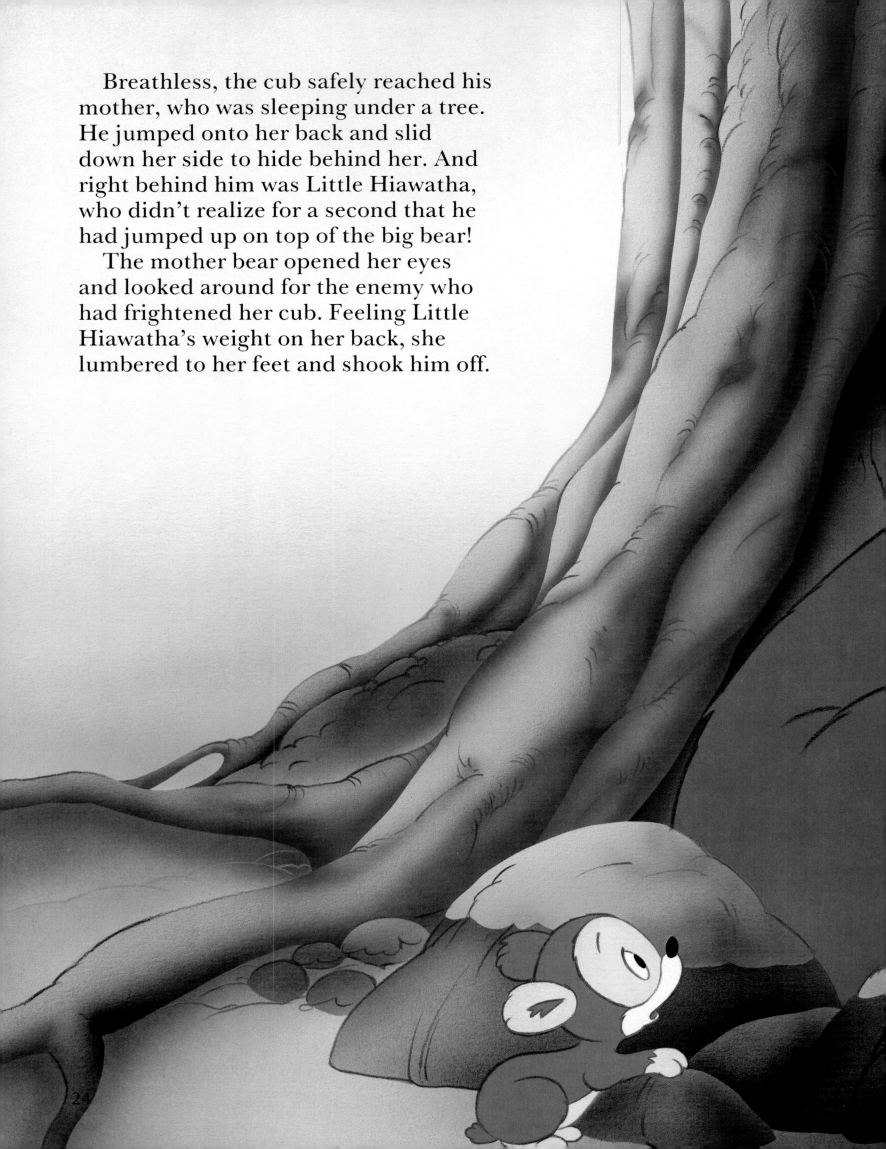

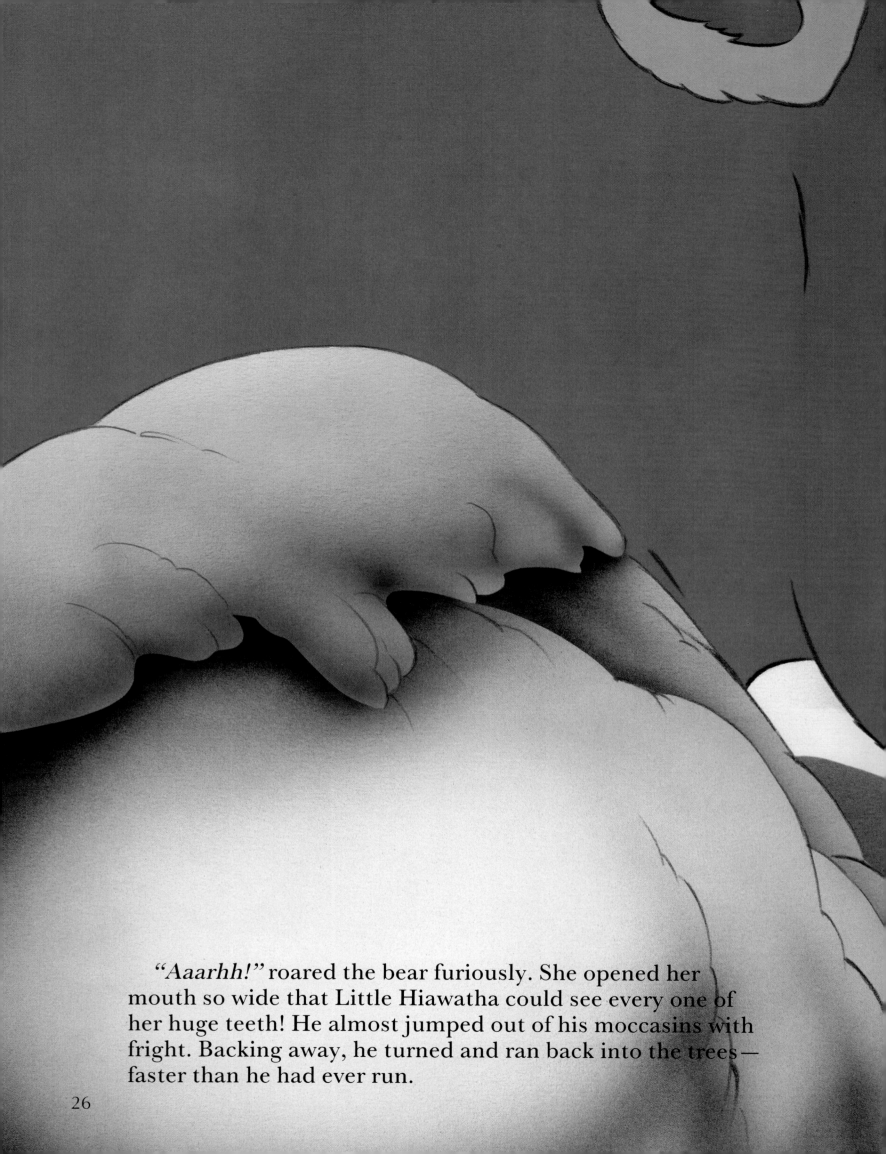

"*Aaarhh!*" roared the bear furiously. She opened her mouth so wide that Little Hiawatha could see every one of her huge teeth! He almost jumped out of his moccasins with fright. Backing away, he turned and ran back into the trees— faster than he had ever run.

The bear stomped angrily after Little Hiawatha, growling and shaking the ground with her footsteps. The noise brought the forest animals out to see what was happening. And there came Little Hiawatha, running for his life! They must do something to help him!

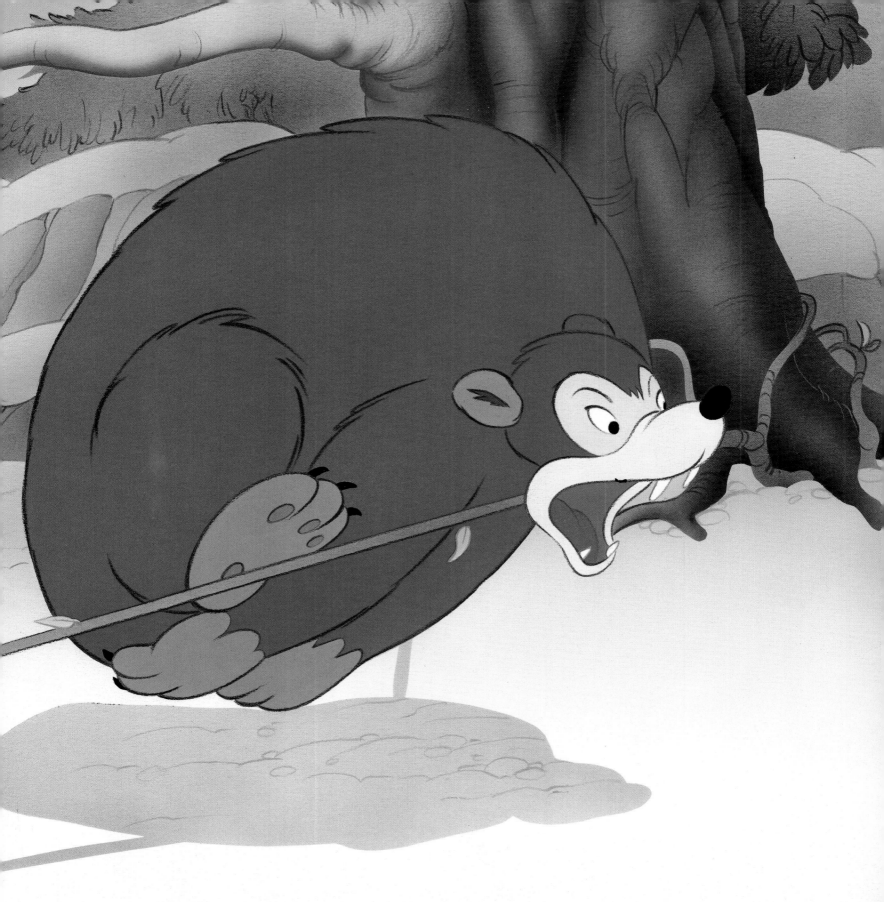

Quickly, three raccoons scampered up a tree, grabbed a long vine, and jumped back down to stretch the vine across the path. When the bear thundered toward them, they pulled the vine tight and tripped her. She rolled end over end, but regained her balance and continued the chase.

Little Hiawatha had followed the path to a stream, where the beavers came to his rescue with a floating log. He jumped onto it, and the beavers paddled toward midstream with their tails, as he wobbled back and forth on the log.

Looking behind him, Little Hiawatha saw the bear charge toward the edge of the stream. He knew the water wouldn't stop her—bears were strong swimmers.

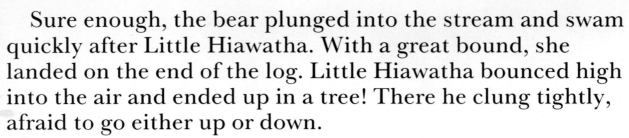

Sure enough, the bear plunged into the stream and swam quickly after Little Hiawatha. With a great bound, she landed on the end of the log. Little Hiawatha bounced high into the air and ended up in a tree! There he clung tightly, afraid to go either up or down.

Then the bear made up his mind for him—she started to climb the tree. He scrambled higher.

Far below, the beavers went to work on the trunk with their sharp teeth. The bear paid no attention, determined to catch up with Little Hiawatha, who was now trapped at the very top of the tree. The tree began to sway, and the beavers gnawed faster. Suddenly, it toppled over!

The bear was about to swat Little Hiawatha with her huge
paw when the tree began to fall. Little Hiawatha clung
desperately to the treetop, but help was near.

A lively possum had climbed the next tree and now swung to the rescue by his tail. At the last moment, he snatched Little Hiawatha from the falling tree! The bear crashed to the ground with a roar.

The rescue had been well planned. Near the cliff's edge, the fawn was waiting with a carrier. When the possum swung by with Little Hiawatha, he dropped him onto the carrier and the fawn sped away. Little Hiawatha hung onto the carrier as tightly as he could, bouncing over the uneven ground.

The light-footed fawn soon outran the mother bear, who was ready to give up the chase, anyway. The sound of her heavy footsteps grew fainter, as the fawn neared the riverbank. What a lot had happened on his first day alone in the woods! But now he was no longer alone. He had made friends who would help him in time of danger—and spread his fame as a woodsman far and wide.

Proudly, Little Hiawatha took his place in the bow of his canoe. The beavers climbed into the stern and began paddling with their tails. Little Hiawatha folded his arms and gazed across the water, thinking of the songs his people would make about him. "Mighty Hiawatha," they would call him, "he who walks the woodland unafraid, friend to every forest creature."

Little Hiawatha smiled as he sped homeward.